Dear Parents:

Congratulations! Your child is taking the first steps on an exciting journey. The destination? Independent reading!

STEP INTO READING® will help your child get there. The program offers five steps to reading success. Each step includes fun stories and colorful art or photographs. In addition to original fiction and books with favorite characters, there are Step into Reading Non-Fiction Readers, Phonics Readers and Boxed Sets, Sticker Readers, and Comic Readers—a complete literacy program with something to interest every child.

Learning to Read, Step by Step!

Ready to Read   Preschool–Kindergarten
• big type and easy words • rhyme and rhythm • picture clues
For children who know the alphabet and are eager to begin reading.

Reading with Help   Preschool–Grade 1
• basic vocabulary • short sentences • simple stories
For children who recognize familiar words and sound out new words with help.

Reading on Your Own   Grades 1–3
• engaging characters • easy-to-follow plots • popular topics
For children who are ready to read on their own.

Reading Paragraphs   Grades 2–3
• challenging vocabulary • short paragraphs • exciting stories
For newly independent readers who read simple sentences with confidence.

Ready for Chapters   Grades 2–4
• chapters • longer paragraphs • full-color art
For children who want to take the plunge into chapter books but still like colorful pictures.

STEP INTO READING® is designed to give every child a successful reading experience. The grade levels are only guides; children will progress through the steps at their own speed, developing confidence in their reading.

Remember, a lifetime love of reading starts with a single step!

For shark fans everywhere!
—B.W.

 Published in the United States by Random House Children's Books, a division of Penguin Random House LLC, 1745 Broadway, New York, NY 10019, and in Canada by Penguin Random House Canada Limited, Toronto.

Visit us on the Web!
StepIntoReading.com
randomhousekids.com
dckids.kidswb.com

Educators and librarians, for a variety of teaching tools, visit us at RHTeachersLibrarians.com

ISBN 978-0-399-55846-7 (trade) — ISBN 978-0-399-55847-4 (lib. bdg.)
ISBN 978-0-399-55848-1 (ebook)

Printed in the United States of America

10 9 8 7 6 5 4 3

DC SUPER FRIENDS™

SHARK ATTACK!

by Billy Wrecks

illustrated by Erik Doescher

Random House 🏠 New York

A space probe falls
from the sky.

It crashes into the sea.
Batman and Aquaman
dive to get it back.

The villain Black Manta
beats them to
the space probe.

He will use it to make
his shark-control device
more powerful.

The hammerhead snaps.

The great white charges.

The tiger shark circles,

protecting Black Manta.

Aquaman tries to talk
to the sharks.
But Black Manta's device
stops him.

The great white
bumps Batman.
It circles back
to take a bite!

Batman barely escapes.

He swims away.

The great white
chases Batman.
Its mouth is filled
with many rows of teeth.

Batman has an idea.
He will lead the shark
to Black Manta.

Aquaman hides
in tall sea grass.
The hammerhead's
wide head
has sensors.

It uses the sensors
to find Aquaman.
The hero calls some fish
to distract the shark!

The school of fish
swirls around
Black Manta, too.
"Go away!" he yells.

The great white
chases Batman.
Black Manta does not
see them coming.

The great white
bumps Black Manta.
The shark-control device
is knocked off his arm!

Batman knows
tiger sharks will try
to eat anything.
The tiger shark
bites the device!

"What have you done?"

Black Manta growls.

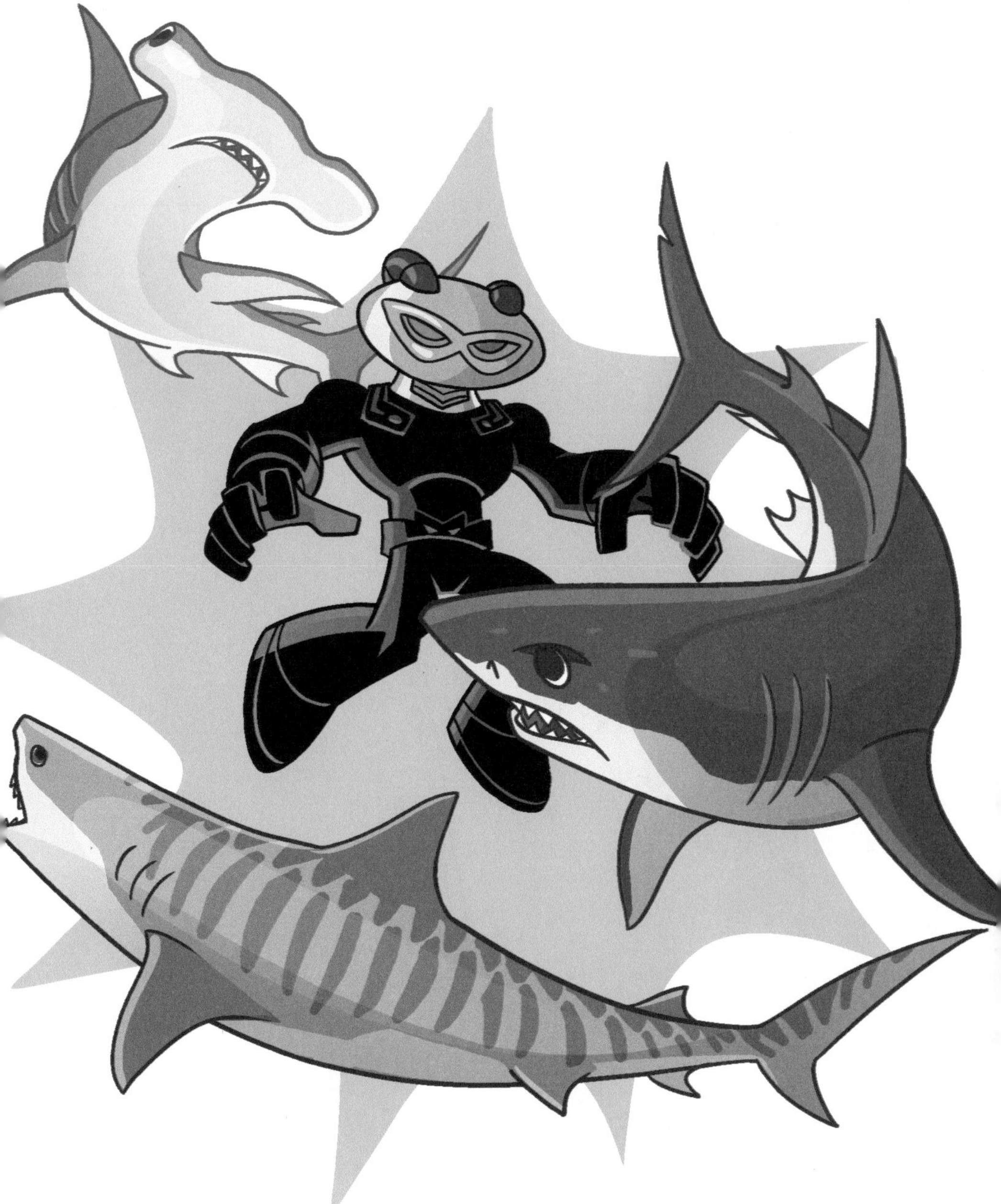

Now the villain cannot control the sharks.

The sharks chase
Black Manta.
Aquaman asks them
not to bite.

Batman calls
the Coast Guard.

"Thank you, friends,"
Aquaman tells the sharks.
"You took a big bite out
of Black Manta's plans!"

Tiger sharks get their name from the stripes along their bodies.

The great white gets its name from its pale underbelly.

Tiger sharks will bite just about anything to see if it can be a meal.

Evidence suggests that sharks have existed for over 420 million years.

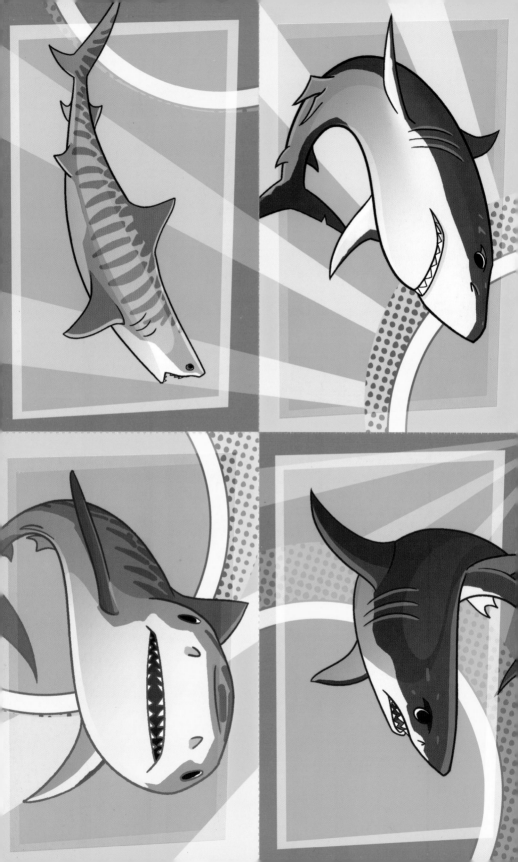

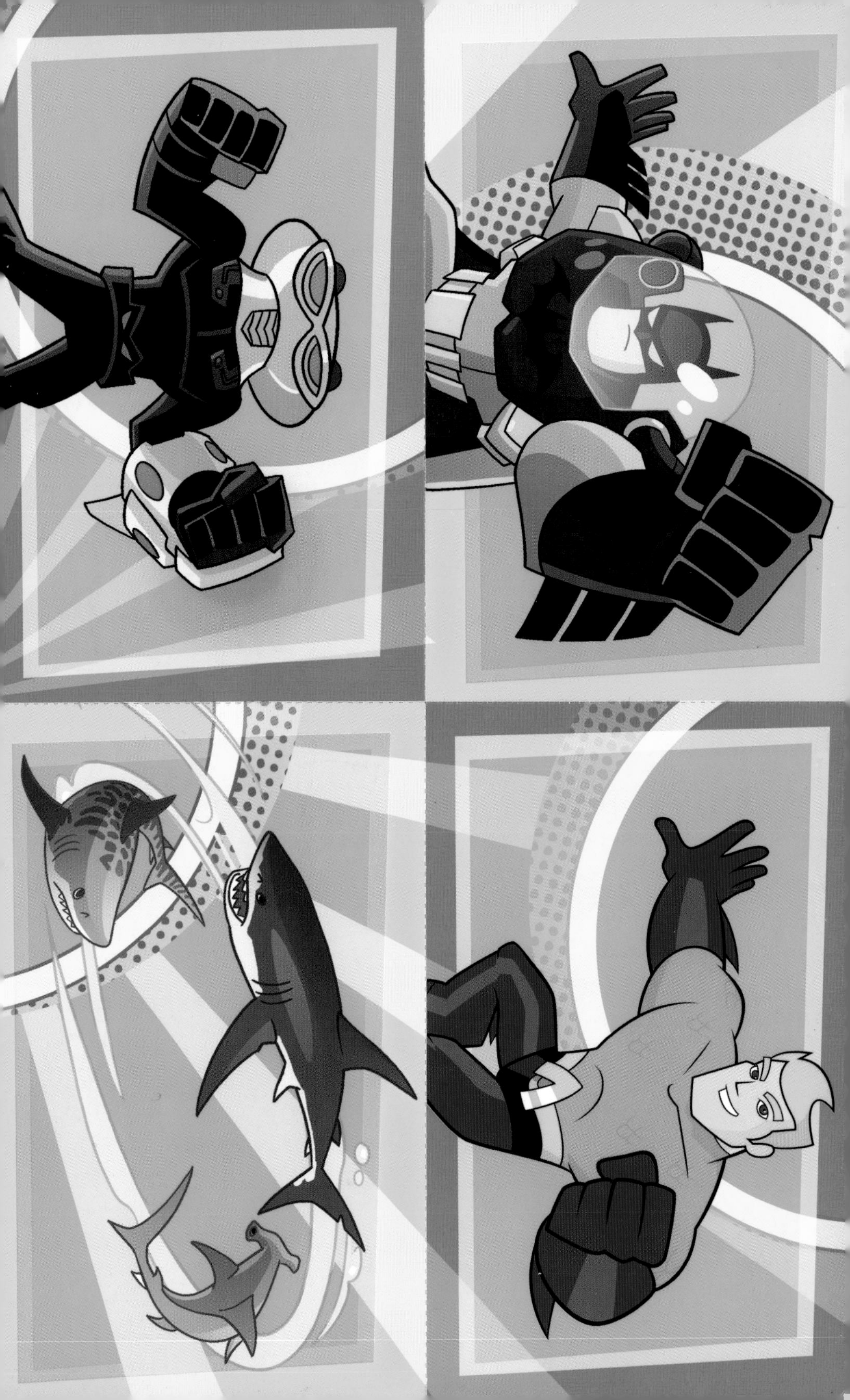

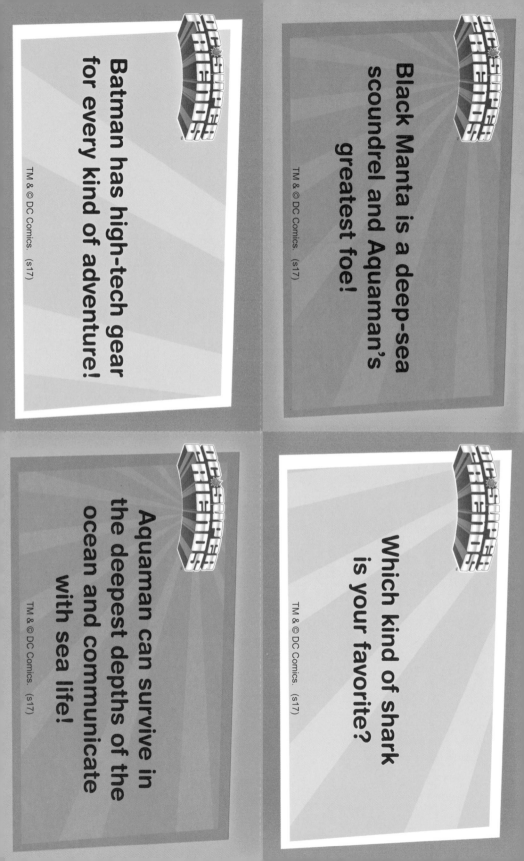

Black Manta is a deep-sea scoundrel and Aquaman's greatest foe!

Which kind of shark is your favorite?

TM & © DC Comics. (s17)

Batman has high-tech gear for every kind of adventure!

TM & © DC Comics. (s17)

Aquaman can survive in the deepest depths of the ocean and communicate with sea life!

TM & © DC Comics. (s17)